WE ARE THE RESISTANCE

By Elizabeth Schaefer

Illustrated by Alan Batson

 A GOLDEN BOOK • NEW YORK

 Published in the United States by Golden Books, an imprint of Random House Children's Books, a division of Penguin Random House LLC, 1745 Broadway, New York, NY 10019, and in Canada by Penguin Random House Canada Limited, Toronto. Golden Books, A Golden Book, A Little Golden Book, the G colophon, and the distinctive gold spine are registered trademarks of Penguin Random House LLC.

rhcbooks.com

ISBN 978-0-593-11836-8 (trade) — ISBN 978-0-593-11837-5 (ebook)

Printed in the United States of America

10 9 8 7 6 5 4 3 2 1

We are the Resistance.

We fight to free the galaxy from the evil First Order.

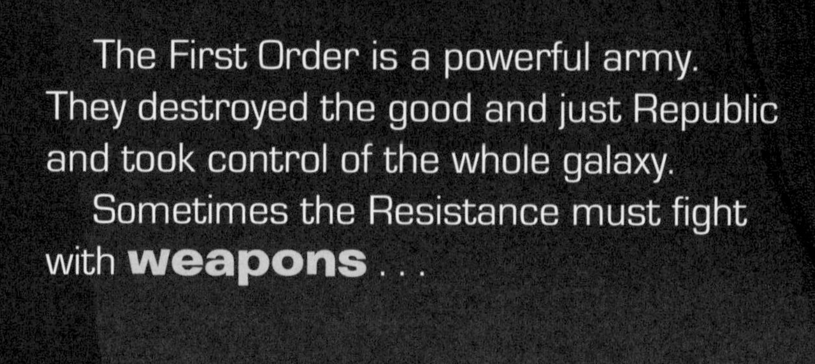

The First Order is a powerful army. They destroyed the good and just Republic and took control of the whole galaxy.

Sometimes the Resistance must fight with **weapons** . . .

. . . but they also fight with their **words** and **actions**. They show others how to stand up for what is right.

Finn was a stormtrooper who chose to leave the First Order and help Resistance pilot **Poe**, even though it was the only life he had ever known.

And the scavenger **Rey** helped the lost droid **BB-8** complete his mission for the Resistance.

The Resistance is **brave**, **loyal**, and **kind**. They work to help those in need, like when **Rose** freed the fathiers on Canto Bight.

The Resistance always
stands up to bullies.

And when all hope seems lost, they **never give up**.

Big or small, the Resistance makes **friends** wherever they go.

Chewbacca befriended little creatures called **porgs**, and **BB-8** made a new friend named **D-O**.

The Resistance welcomes **everyone**, no matter where they are from or what they look like.

The First Order uses **hatred** and **fear** to control the galaxy.

And their weapons are **big** and **powerful**.

But the Resistance always **fights hard**, even when facing overwhelming odds.

The Resistance strives to protect the galaxy. From the **hottest** deserts . . .

. . . to the **coldest** reaches of space.

The Resistance races into
battle with **old allies** . . .

. . . and tries to recruit others to **join in the fight**, like **Zorii** and **Jannah**.

Sometimes the galaxy can seem
dark and frightening.

But with loyal friends at their side,
these heroes have everything they need.
We are the Resistance!